# BUG BUDDIES

## Beetle Power!

*With special thanks to Mariam Vossough*

*To my bug buddies Lily and Sol*

First published in paperback in Great Britain by
HarperCollins *Children's Books* in 2009
HarperCollins *Children's Books* is a division of HarperCollins *Publishers* Ltd,
77-85 Fulham Palace Road, Hammersmith, London W6 8JB.

Visit our website at: www.harpercollins.co.uk

1 3 5 7 9 10 8 6 4 2

Text copyright © Working Partners 2009
Illustrations copyright © Duncan Smith 2009

ISBN-13: 978-0-00-732247-3

Printed and bound in England by Clays Ltd, St Ives plc

# BUG BUDDIES

## Beetle Power!

## JOE MILLER

**Illustrated by Duncan Smith**

HarperCollins *Children's Books*

Spinner's Wood
is full of sticky mud, tall trees
and long grass. But most of
all, it's full of bugs! Now, some
people think that bugs are pests.
But they haven't met Gonzo or
the **Bug Buddies** – four best
friends called **Zap, Buzz,
Lurch** and **Crunch**. Their life
would be perfect if it wasn't
for a spider called **Spinner**,
who has eight legs and one
mission: to trap the whole wood
in his evil web. But you'll
soon find out that even
bugs can be heroes...

# Contents

# CHAPTER 1

Zap was about to score! He darted towards the empty goal and nudged the grass seed ball forwards, ready to shoot. Suddenly Crunch took up position between the two goalposts. The huge stag beetle spread out his claws.

*Slimy snails!* thought Zap. *How am I going to get the ball past him?*

Then he had an idea. He zipped underneath Crunch's shiny black body, between his legs and out the other side.

"Where's Zap gone?" said Crunch, peering between his legs.

"Here I am!" shouted Zap, nudging the ball into the goal.

Zap flew into the air, doing a loop-the-loop in celebration. He may be the smallest beetle in Spinner's Wood – but he was faster than the rest of his Bug Buddies.

"Nice move," Buzz the ladybird called. Zap landed on the soft grass. His best friend, Lurch the dung beetle, scuttled over to him.

"I've seen beetles crawl *over* somebody to score," he said, "but never underneath!"

"I told you this was a good place for a game of Beetle Ball," said Buzz. "The short grass makes it perfect for Zap's fancy moves."

"We can play here now that we don't have to worry about Spinner," said Crunch.

A tingle of nerves ran through Zap. The Bug Buddies never usually played Beetle Ball this close to Shadow Creek. But since the evil spider, Spinner, had been trapped in a tunnel a few weeks ago, everyone in Spinner's Wood had lived peacefully. Zap still kept an eye out for eight hairy legs, though.

*After all*, he thought, *we've defeated Spinner before and he's* **always** *returned.*

The four friends made their way over to Algae Pond. "Playing Beetle Ball has made me hungry," said Buzz.

Zap laughed. "*Everything* makes you hungry!" he said.

Buzz crawled off to search for a snack. Zap smiled as a group of pond-skaters glided over on the surface of the water. Their thin, brown bodies were held above the

 13

water by four long, skinny legs.

"I wish we could play you at Beetle Ball," one of them called.

"Me too," said Zap, "but we can't float on water."

"I wonder if dung balls float?" said Lurch.

Zap chuckled. His best friend was forever talking about poo!

A pond-skater pointed a leg towards the other side of the pond. "Hey," he said, "I didn't know ladybirds could actually *make* things go spotty."

14

Zap saw Buzz sitting on a rock which was covered in small, black spots.

"Time to play a trick," said Zap, mischievously.

Zap, Lurch and Crunch flew across the pond, landing next to Buzz.

"Oh no," said Zap, pointing at the rock, "are you losing your spots?"

Buzz spat out his snack.

"My spots! Pick them up, quick!"

He started scrabbling around on the rock.

"I'm only teasing," said Zap. "Your

spots can't *really* fall off. Anyway,
you don't have this many. You've
only got seven, remember?"

Lurch scuttled across the rock,
examining the dark spots with a
worried expression on his face.

"What's wrong?" asked Zap.

"We'd better be on the lookout
for more of these," said Lurch.

"Why?" asked Crunch. "They're
just a bunch of spots."

"Depends on who left them here,"
said Lurch.

Zap felt a prickle of anxiety.

 17

When something mysterious happened near Shadow Creek, it usually meant that a certain spider was up to no good...

# CHAPTER 2

The Bug Buddies flew through the
wood, searching for more dark
spots.

**"There's some!"** shouted Zap,
pointing to a green and white hosta
plant on the edge of a small clearing.

Lurch swooped down on the fat

leaves, dashing from spot to spot,

peering at each one.

"Look," said Buzz, pointing his

antennae. "They're all along the

bank, too."

Zap looked round to see a trail of

spots heading towards Gonzo's

Rock. Lurch hurried over to the trail.

He flew faster as he came across

more and more spots.

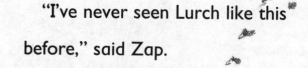

"I've never seen Lurch like this

before," said Zap.

"Me neither," said Crunch,

sounding nervous.

21

Lurch crawled back towards them, with a very worried look on his face. "Gather round," he whispered.

Zap huddled in close to his Bug Buddies.

"Why are you whispering?" asked Buzz.

Lurch nodded at a group of yellow butterflies and white moths playing happily nearby. "I know what the spots are," said the dung

beetle, "and I don't want to scare the whole wood."

Zap's tummy did a nervous flip. "It's Spinner, isn't it?" he said.

"Shh!" said Lurch. He nodded slowly. "Yes, it's Spinner. Those dark spots are spider poo."

Zap's wings drooped – this was terrible news.

"Are you s-sure?" said Crunch, his big claws clattering together.

"If there's one thing I'm sure about," said Lurch, "it's poo."

"I *knew* he'd be back," said Zap.

"It's not just Spinner," said Lurch. "With this much poo, he must have an army of spiders with him!"

"We need to tell Gonzo," said Zap, flapping his wings. **"Right now!"**

Zap spotted the wise grasshopper sitting on his rock. He landed next to Gonzo, his friends following close behind.

"We've got some news for you," he said gravely. "Spinner's back."

Gonzo nodded his head, slowly. He didn't look surprised.

*I wasn't the only one who expected Spinner to return*, Zap thought.

"And he's got squillions of other spiders with him," said Lurch. "There's spider poo everywhere."

"Look – it's all around your rock," said Crunch, inspecting the slab that Gonzo was sat on. "We're in danger!"

"If Spinner was going to attack us, he'd have done it by now," said Gonzo, calmly. "He must be busy hatching his latest plan."

"What are we going to do?" asked Zap.

Gonzo took a deep breath. "It's time to end this feud. Ask all our insect friends to meet here when the sun is highest in the sky," he replied.

"I'm going to make the most important speech Spinner's Wood has ever heard."

# CHAPTER 3

Zap and his friends spread the news about Gonzo's meeting. They visited every friendly bug in the wood, from the earwigs on Rotten Row to the dragonflies over at Soggy Bog.

Zap felt the sun beam down on his wings – it was already high in the sky.

"We should head back," he said, "or we'll be the only ones not at the meeting!"

Zap couldn't believe his eyes as he flew into the clearing by Gonzo's Rock. It was packed! Insects who were usually sworn enemies stood side by side, waiting to hear what Gonzo had to say.

"I never thought I'd see Mac the caterpillar standing next to Stig the wasp," said Lurch.

"Me neither," said Buzz. "They hate each other!"

 29

Zap found the last clear patch of ground for them to land on. Buzz, Crunch and Lurch crawled to the front. Zap flew upwards, hovering

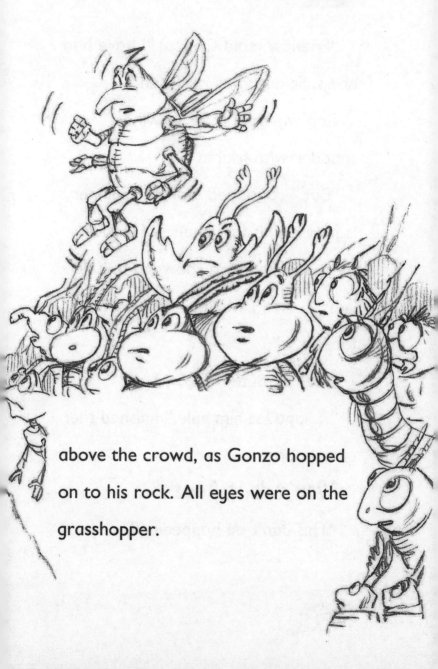

above the crowd, as Gonzo hopped

on to his rock. All eyes were on the

grasshopper.

"Friends," said Gonzo. "I have bad news. Spinner has returned."

Zap watched rows of wings shudder with fright.

"But," continued Gonzo, "Spinner is now on his last chance. He must be challenged to a showdown. If he wins... then I will leave the wood forever..."

"No!" shouted Zap.

"... and let him rule," finished the grasshopper.

**"Don't do it, Gonzo!"**

"This can't be happening!"

Cries filled the clearing and Gonzo lifted his front legs in a plea for quiet.

"If Spinner loses," said the grasshopper, "then he must agree to be ruled by me and live peacefully among us. I wish I could be the one to fight this last battle, but I'm too old. So, one of you must step up to the challenge as my champion."

Zap's antennae prickled with nerves as he looked around the crowd, waiting for some big

courageous bug to raise his or her wing. But most of them looked at the ground, shuffling their legs.

Zap sensed he was being watched. He turned to see the grasshopper gazing at him. Out of all the bugs here, *he* was the one Gonzo was looking at. Zap might be the smallest bug in the wood, but Gonzo often told him that he was the bravest.

*This is it*, thought Zap. *This is what he's been training me for.*

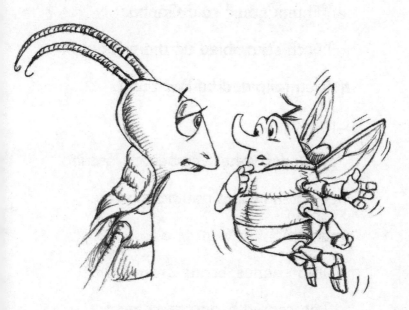

Zap took a deep breath and flew up next to the grasshopper. **"I'll do it,"** he said. "Even if I have to face Spinner alone."

The crowd gasped.

 35

"Thank you," said Gonzo.

Lurch scrambled up the rock, quickly followed by Buzz and Crunch.

"You daft weevil," said Lurch. "As if we're going to let you do this by yourself!"

"No chance," said Crunch.

The crowd began to cheer.

### "Bug Buddies are the best,"

cried Willy the wasp beetle.

"Spinner doesn't stand a chance!" shouted Mazie the millipede.

Zap felt proud to have such loyal

friends. But he wondered whether the Bug Buddies had taken on too much this time.

"What have I got us into?" he said to himself, as a group of ants crawled over to wish them good luck.

After all, Spinner would do *anything* to become leader of the wood. Could they really stop him?

# CHAPTER 4

When everyone had finished wishing
them good luck, Zap turned to the
other Bug Buddies.

"We need to work out how we're
going to find Spinner," he said.
"We've flown all over the wood
today and didn't see him once."

"I'll try my best to find his trail," said Lurch. "But he and his spider friends have pooped everywhere!"

Gonzo pointed towards the space in front of the crowd.

"Say hello to my relatives," he said, "the speckled bush crickets."

Zap watched as a group of bugs suddenly appeared and crawled up on to the rock. They had plump, grass-green bodies with a brown stripe down their backs. Their long, wispy antennae swayed in the breeze.

39

"Pleased to meet you, sir," said a cricket, lifting his front leg to salute Zap. "I'm Sergeant Stealth."

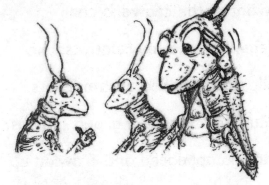

"The crickets can camouflage themselves, so they're perfect detectives," said Gonzo. "And detective skills are just what you need to find that spider."

"Great," said Zap, smiling at the crickets. "The more help, the better."

Captain Drone, leader of the bees, flew forward. "My bees can safeguard the bugs from attack while you're gone," he said.

Snap, the leader of the green tiger beetles, waved his legs from the back of the crowd.

"And the tiger beetles will help too," he called.

"Thanks," said Zap, pleased to know everyone was in safe hands. **"OK, Bug Buddies, let's go!"**

With cheers from the crowd, the Bug Buddies and the crickets headed off. Lurch led the way, hurriedly following the black spots through the grass. The bush crickets moved silently alongside the Bug Buddies.

"I never thought I'd be following poo through the wood," said Buzz, disgusted.

"We're honorary dung beetles for the day!" joked Zap.

42

They were about to enter a patch of shrubs when Lurch stopped.

"The trail has run dry," he said. Then his antennae pricked up. "What's that squeaking sound?"

The crickets rushed into the shrubs to investigate, their camouflage making them instantly disappear.

Zap and his friends glanced at each other, then waited patiently by the shrubs.

It wasn't long before Sergeant Stealth and the crickets returned,

along with a group of baby mice.

Their tiny, pink ears were almost

hidden beneath their fluffy, white fur.

"Tell them what you saw,"

said Sergeant Stealth.

"He was so b-b-big," squeaked a

tiny mouse.

"Eyes as black as n-n-night," squeaked another.

**"Sounds like Spinner!"** exclaimed Crunch.

"Perhaps it's not such a good idea to find him," said the smallest cricket, his antennae shaking.

"We can't turn back," said Zap. "The future of the wood is at stake!"

"He's right," said Sergeant Stealth. "Crickets never abandon a mission."

Sergeant Stealth and the other crickets pointed the baby mice back in the direction of their nest.

"Er, where have they gone?" said Crunch, after a moment.

Zap looked round, but the crickets were nowhere to be seen. Their camouflage was working *too* well. The Bug Buddies had lost the rest of their team.

"Quick," Zap said. "Spread out! Find which way they went."

Zap flew to the far end of the shrubs. He searched behind every plant and leaf. Suddenly, he felt a sharp tap on his shoulder. It wasn't one of the Bug Buddies, because he

could see them up ahead, searching

in another patch of grass.

Zap gulped. *Had a nasty spider*

*crept up behind him?*

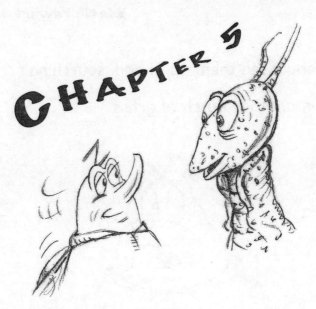

# CHAPTER 5

Zap's heart pounded as he slowly
turned round. His wings drooped
with relief when he saw the crickets
standing behind him.

"Thank goodness, it's you!" Zap
cried. "Where did you go?"

"We were taking the baby mice

back when we spotted some gossiping money spiders," said Sergeant Stealth. "So, we sneaked up and listened in on their conversation. It was very interesting."

Buzz, Lurch and Crunch crawled over to join them.

"Was Spinner there too?" asked Zap.

"No," said Sergeant Stealth. "But we found out where he's hiding – Stinking Bog."

Zap shared a worried look with the Bug Buddies. Apart from

 49

Shadow Creek, Stinking Bog was the smelliest, scariest place in Spinner's Wood.

"But Gonzo has always told us to avoid the bog," said Crunch, nervously.

"I'm afraid we've got no choice," said Zap.

The smell almost knocked Zap over. "Now I know why it's called Stinking Bog," he said.

It hadn't taken the team of crickets and bugs long to get there. All they had to do was follow the pong…

"It's revolting!" said Buzz, his legs wobbling like he was going to faint.

Crunch used his giant claw to waft the smell away from Buzz.

"Mmm… it smells just like my breakfast!" said Lurch, smiling.

"Yum!"

"Yes," cried Buzz. "But you eat *poo*!"

**"And I eat beetles!"** cried a hissing voice from above.

Zap looked up to see a thick strand of silk hanging from a branch. Lowering himself down on it was

Spinner – looking bigger and meaner than ever.

"The only question is," said Spinner, "which one of you shall I eat first?"

The giant spider landed on a rock in the middle of the bog, spreading out his thick hairy legs. Zap shivered. How could they take on this monster and win?

Zap crawled forward, trying hard to stop his wings trembling.

"Ah," smiled Spinner, "are you volunteering to be the first inside

my stomach?"

"No," said Zap, "I'm challenging you to a final showdown."

Spinner burst out laughing. "You what?!" he said.

"This is your last chance," continued Zap. "If we win, then you will promise to live by Gonzo's rules and respect the life of every bug in Spinner's Wood. But if you win… Gonzo has agreed to leave the wood forever."

Spinner immediately stopped laughing. His eyes lit up. "In that

case," Spinner said, "it will be my
pleasure. But if you have friends to
help you, it's only fair that I do too."

Zap watched as hundreds of
spiders crawled out from behind
every rock in Stinking Bog.

Everywhere he looked, beady eyes stared at him. **They were surrounded!**

# CHAPTER 6

"We're doomed!" cried Crunch.

"There are enough of us to put up a fight," said Zap, bravely. "Isn't that right, Sergeant Stealth?"

Zap turned to the crickets, but was shocked to see that they were no longer there.

"Those cowardly crickets have

crept off!" cried Buzz.

"They've done their job in helping us to find Spinner," said Zap. "It's *our* job to take him on."

"But there's only four of us. There are **loads** of them," said Lurch. He pointed towards the swarm of spiders, flexing their legs.

"Yes," said Zap, standing as tall as he could. "But we're the Bug Buddies. We've defeated Spinner before – **we can do it again!**"

With Zap leading the way, the Bug Buddies crawled forward.

 **59**

A group of small spiders shot out strands of silk to trip them up.

"**Ouch!**" cried Lurch, falling flat on his face.

Zap zoomed into the air. "I'll see to this lot," he shouted down to the others. "You battle your way to Spinner."

Zap flew round and round above the spiders. Silky strands shot towards him, but he quickly darted out of the way. As they fell to the ground, the webs tangled around the spiders. *My plan's working*, he thought.

Zap flew faster and faster as the spiders continued to fire their sticky strands. They were so busy trying to fire at him, the spiders didn't realise they were tying themselves up in webs!

"That's one-nil to us," said Zap, smiling.

He flew over to join his friends. Crunch had taken the lead, waving his giant claws to clear a path through their attackers. Behind him, Lurch was lobbing dung balls at the advancing spiders.

Buzz was sucking up grass seeds, then firing them out of his mouth at the spiders. Most of the smaller ones scuttled away, as the hard, round balls bounced off their bodies. Spinner hissed as his army backed off towards the wood, leaving a large gap in front of him.

"Nice work!" said Zap, hovering above them. "We've cleared a path through to Spinner."

Buzz sucked up some more seeds and blew as hard as he could.

**"Ow, ow, ow, ow, ow!"** cried Spinner, as five grass seeds hit his head, one after another.

The giant spider fell over, looking dazed. *Now's our chance*, thought Zap. He whizzed round to the back of Spinner and gave the spider's body a nip.

"That hurt, you sneaky bug," cried Spinner.

The huge spider kicked out a leg, but Zap easily dodged out of the way. Excitement made his wings flutter even faster. Spinner was down and his spider friends had retreated. It looked like the battle was going their way...

"Help!"

Zap whipped his head round to see
Lurch stuck in the mud, surrounded
by taunting spiders. Zap gasped – his
friend was sinking! He zoomed across
and grabbed one of Lurch's legs. Zap
pulled and pulled, but he wasn't
strong enough to free the dung beetle.
What was he going to do?

Crunch rushed over, elbowing the spiders out of the way. "Let me try," he said, hooking his giant claws around the dung beetle's body. He began to lift him, his body trembling with the effort.

**"Get off me, you sneaky beasts!"** cried Buzz from the other side of the bog.

Zap saw that a group of spiders were trying to pin Buzz down with their webs.

Spinner got to his feet, laughing with delight. "It looks like the Bug

Buddies are about to be defeated,"

he said. **"Say goodbye, Gonzo!"**

Was Spinner really going to win?

# CHAPTER 7

"I'll be OK, Zap," Buzz called over, bravely fighting off the spiders. "Get Spinner!"

Zap flew up into the air and headed straight for his giant enemy. **"I'll never let you take over the wood,"** he shouted.

Spinner smiled, venom dripping off his fangs. "How can one lone weevil possibly stop me?" he said.

Zap gulped. What *could* he do?

"The thing is," cried a voice from above, "he's *not* alone."

Zap looked up to see Crunch and Lurch in the branches of a horse chestnut tree. Lurch was covered in mud, but he was free again! Crunch was using his claws to cut loose a bunch of heavy tree buds. With one last snip, the buds were free. Zap gasped as they came hurtling

 69

towards him. He dodged out of the
way as the buds skimmed past his
wings and landed with a CRACK on
Spinner's head.

"Bang… head… hurty," said
Spinner, dazed.

Lurch threw a hail of
dung balls at the
stunned spider. "Take that!"
he shouted. The stinky,
brown poo
splattered all
over Spinner's
hairy legs.

"**Argh**," shouted Spinner,

confused about where the volley of

poo was coming from. "You little

pests won't give up!"

"Never!" cried Zap.

"Unlike your so-called friends," shouted Buzz from the other side of the bog.

The spiders that were surrounding Buzz had run away. All across the bog, frightened spiders were abandoning Spinner.

"Come back!" shouted Spinner. "The fight's not lost yet."

Zap smiled as Buzz flew up to join him.

"I'm glad *my friends* would never desert me," Zap said.

"No way," mumbled Buzz, his mouth full of grass seeds. He quickly fired the seeds at Spinner, hitting him square in the face.

"Ouch!" yelled Spinner, crumpling to the ground.

*Right*, thought Zap, *now we'll see him off for good.* Zap dived towards Spinner and flew round his huge body, giving him nip after nip.

**"Will you – ow – stop – ow – biting me? I give in!"** yelled Spinner.

Buzz, Crunch and Lurch joined

73

Zap, hovering side by side in front of
the defeated spider.

Spinner curled up on the ground
covered in tree buds, grass seeds
and poo.

"You've lost," said Zap. "Now you
have to obey Gonzo's rules and live
in peace and harmony with all bugs."

Spinner laughed, louder than the Bug Buddies had ever heard him laugh before. "Me? Behave myself?" he said.

"You promised," said Zap, angrily.

"When will you understand?" said Spinner. "Spiders are hunters. It's what we were born to do. We don't follow rules."

With a sudden effort, Spinner shook himself free of the sticky mess. "I'm going to find a new home. Some place where no little pests can foil my plans!"

Zap watched as Spinner shot a strand of silk high up into the horse chestnut tree and flew into the air. A gust of wind blew him far away, past the trees of Spinner's Wood and out into the world beyond.

"We won! Spinner's gone for good," said Crunch.

"And Gonzo doesn't have to leave," said Buzz.

**"Go Bug Buddies!"** cried Lurch.

Zap wing-slapped his Bug Buddies. The wood was safe at last.

# CHAPTER 8

"Let's go and tell Gonzo the good news," said Zap.

The Bug Buddies were just about to leave Stinking Bog when they heard a disgusting squelch. A huge slug emerged from the mud. Its thick, mucus-covered body slithered up to Zap, leaving a trail of slime.

Zap shuddered – that was one ugly

creature…

"I sssaw what you and your friendsss

did," the slug said. "Very impressssive."

Even though the slug was

congratulating them, it didn't sound

like he meant it.

"Er, thanks," Zap said. "My

name's Zap."

"Yesss," replied the slug,

menacingly, "I know."

"We're going to celebrate our victory,"

said Lurch. "Do you want to come?"

 79

"No, thanksss," replied the slug.

"I'm, er, busy… very busy."

Zap thought the slug's excuse

sounded like a fib. He was suddenly

keen to get away from this slippery

character.

"OK," Zap said hurriedly, "bye, then."

Zap flew out of the bog, followed by the rest of the Bug Buddies. As he led the way, he took one last look over his wings. The slug was still watching them…

The insects of Spinner's Wood cheered as Zap and his friends told everyone about their victory, on Gonzo's Rock.

**"Spinner has left the wood forever!"** Zap announced.

"Well done, Bug Buddies," said Gonzo.

"It was a real team effort," said Zap, looking at his friends with pride.

**"Hooray for the Bug Buddies!"** the crowd cheered.

Zap smiled as Buzz, Crunch and Lurch were lifted up by the bugs at the front of the crowd and carried around the clearing. But, before Zap could celebrate, there was something he needed to know.

"Would you really have left Spinner's Wood?" he asked Gonzo.

"I knew that promising to leave was the only way Spinner would ever agree to a final showdown," replied Gonzo. "But, I also knew that you wouldn't let me down."

Zap almost burst with pride. Suddenly, he felt himself lifted into the air...

"Don't be shy," said Snap, putting Zap on his shoulders. "You deserve a victory lap, too!"

Zap laughed as the tiger beetle

carried him around the clearing. It
was almost as fun as flying!

But his laughter paused when he
spotted the giant slug watching him
from behind a muddy mound. *What*

*was he doing here? Didn't he say he was*

*busy?*

Zap wasn't sure why, but something told him to keep an eye on that slug. He reminded Zap of Spinner in some way.

"I don't think our adventures are over yet," he murmured to himself, as he joined in with the celebrations. "Not by a long way… "

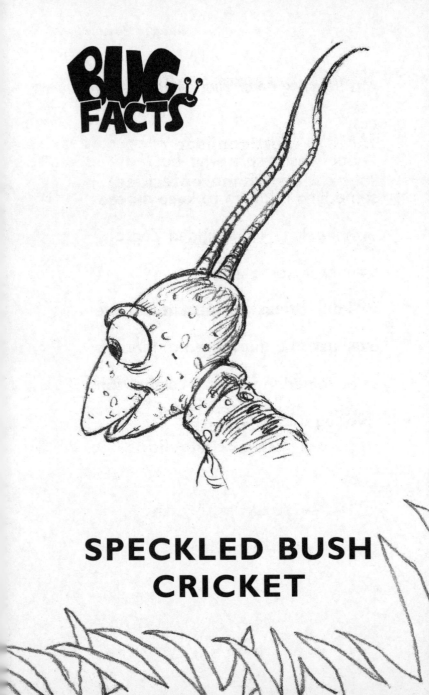

**SPECKLED BUSH CRICKET**

**NAME:** Sergeant Stealth

**FAMILY:** Tettigoniidae
(sub-family: Phaneropteridae)

**SIZE:** Average 15mm

**HOME:** Meadows, gardens and orchards

**LIKES:** Eating leaves and flowers of plants such as dandelions.

**DISLIKES:** Areas where they cannot be camouflaged!

# SERGEANT STEALTH

Unlike many other species of cricket,
the speckled bush cricket can't fly. The
female has no wings at all, while the male
just has little flaps. It's a good thing they
have long legs to help them hop around!

## Slime Time

There's something sticky going on in Spinner's Wood. Bugs are going missing and a slimy trail is leading straight to Stinking Bog...

## COMING SOON!

Turn over for a sneak preview of book six...

# CHAPTER 1

Zap waved his wings to get Buzz's
attention. He was standing unmarked,
right by Centipede United's goal. If his
friend passed him the apple-pip ball
he could score!

Suddenly, a leaf blew on to the
pitch in front of Buzz. The ladybird

dropped the ball and started
chomping on the juicy snack. Zap's
antenna sagged. They'd never win
now.

"What a time to stop for a nibble!"
said Lurch, darting in and grabbing the
apple pip.

**"Over here!"** shouted Zap.

Lurch hurled the seed in Zap's direction. The clover seed weevil flicked a wing and sent the ball flying straight into Centipede United's goal. Gonzo the grasshopper clicked to signal the end of the match.

**To be continued…**

It's the Beetle Ball final and the Bug Buddies face the mighty Centipede United. But who's lurking on the sidelines? Could it be Spinner?

Spinner's Wood is under attack! The Bug Buddies think a certain spider is up to his old tricks. But is a new enemy on the prowl?

It's party time and the yellow ants are happy to share their yummy food with the Bug Buddies. But is there something funny in the honey? What could the ants be up to...

A storm is coming and scary tiger beetles need shelter. But can the Bug Buddies trust them? And is Spinner really gone for good?

# BUG BUDDIES

## JOE MILLER

Buy more great Bug Buddies books direct from
HarperCollins *Publishers*: at 10% off recommended
retail price. FREE postage and packing in the UK.

| | |
|---|---|
| The Big Game | ISBN: 978-0-00-731039-5 |
| Enemy Attack! | ISBN: 978-0-00-731040-1 |
| Ant Invasion! | ISBN: 978-0-00-731041-8 |
| Tunnel Trouble | ISBN: 978-0-00-731042-5 |
| Beetle Power! | ISBN: 978-0-00-732247-3 |
| Slime Time | ISBN: 978-0-00-732248-0 |

**All priced at £3.99 RRP**

**More books coming soon!**